About the Author

Author, Carrie M. Dale, is a proud graduate of Saint James School and the Arlington High School, both in Arlington Heights, IL. Her early years laid the foundation for this book, as her creative writing teachers always encouraged her. She is currently an Associate Professor at Eastern Illinois University, where she teaches a variety of foundational classes in elementary education.

The Portal

Carrie M. Dale

The Portal

Vanguard Press

VANGUARD PAPERBACK

© Copyright 2023 **Carrie M. Dale**

The right of Carrie M. Dale to be identified as author of this work has been asserted by them in accordance with the Copyright, Designs and Patents Act 1988.

All Rights Reserved

No reproduction, copy or transmission of this publication may be made without written permission.
No paragraph of this publication may be reproduced, copied or transmitted save with the written permission of the publisher, or in accordance with the provisions of the Copyright Act 1956 (as amended).

Any person who commits any unauthorised act in relation to this publication may be liable to criminal prosecution and civil claims for damages.

A CIP catalogue record for this title is available from the British Library.

ISBN 978 1 80016 968 5

Vanguard Press is an imprint of
Pegasus Elliot Mackenzie Publishers Ltd.
www.pegasuspublishers.com

This is a work of fiction. Names, characters, businesses, places, events and incidents are either the product of the author's imagination or are used in a fictitious manner. Any resemblance to actual persons, living or dead, or actual events is purely coincidental.

First Published in 2023

Vanguard Press
Sheraton House Castle Park
Cambridge England

Printed & Bound in Great Britain

Gratefully dedicated to Caroline Schafer, William Welsh (dec.) and Ava Gertrude Dale (dec.)

I am grateful to all who provided support to me during the process of writing this book. Special mention goes to Daiva Markelis and the Sisters of Christian Charity in Wilmette, IL, who fed me while I continued to write. John Titus was instrumental in seeing this book come to completion, as was Terry Coulton.

Chapter 1

I ran as fast as I could up Mulberry Hill. I was out of breath by the time I reached the top. I had grown quite a bit since last summer and my bike was really a little too small for me now. I was on my way to Fisher's Market to buy my mom a pound of butter for the cookies she promised to bake me. Normally, she would have driven to Fisher's and gotten it herself or dropped me off to run inside, but it was a beautiful day, school had just let out for the summer, and I was itching to get out of the house, so I offered to bike here. The streets were not very busy this time of mid-day. I parked my bike, paid for the butter, and headed home. I could almost taste those cookies already.

It wasn't long before the smell drew me out of my bedroom and down the hall into the kitchen. Mom poured me a big glass of cold milk and gave me three warm cookies off the rack. My mouth watered. They were delicious.

"We're having a late dinner tonight, Mykayla," my mom said. "Your father must finish up the school year at the office and will be home later than usual. So, enjoy your snack. Are you going over to Junie's house this afternoon?"

"Yeah. She leaves this weekend, so I want to see her as much as I can before she goes."

"Well, don't forget about Mrs Ferguson's list!" my mom reminded me.

Mrs Ferguson was my fourth-grade teacher this past year. She gave us a list of books we should read over the summer before we went into fifth grade. After much moaning and groaning, we looked at the 'list', only to discover there were only four books on it, and they didn't seem that bad. My mom thought I should start right away, but, of course, I wanted to wait 'until later'. Junie is my best friend, and we were in Mrs Ferguson's class together, and we really hoped we would be assigned to the same class in fifth grade. But it was too early in the summer to know that yet. One thing I wasn't looking forward to this summer was Junie going away for most of it. Her family always vacationed in Mississippi with her grandparents almost all summer long, which meant we were reduced to texting, phone calls and letter-writing. It just wasn't the same as having her just down the street or having her over for sleepovers. I was afraid it was going to be another lonely summer.

Of course, I have my parents and they are okay. My mom is a dentist in town and my dad is the principal at the high school. I don't have any brothers or sisters, which makes me sad, but last year I finally wore my mom down and she got me the dog I always wanted. I named her Roxy, and she is a sweet little mutt of a thing. She sleeps with me and everything. I am responsible for feeding her, walking her, and cleaning up after her. That was a bigger job when she was younger; it is easier now that she is a little older and better trained. I even taught her some tricks! My dad likes to tell the story of when I was really little and how I kept asking repeatedly for a pony. I don't remember doing that, but I do think horses are cool, though we could never own one where we currently live. Course I understand that now, but probably didn't back then!

***

Junie's family just left. It was a tearful goodbye for the two of us, and even though we promised to keep in touch, we know it won't be the same. My mom wants me to help her clean out some closets in the house (not fun) and my dad wants me to help him clean out the garage (more not fun). I want to just get on my bike and ride. Actually, I want to get a NEW bike and ride, because I truthfully have outgrown my current bike. I must be going through a growth spurt or something, because my summer clothes don't fit me so well any more, either. Maybe I can talk my mom into taking me shopping at the mall on her day off... now THAT would be fun. In the meantime, I have the whole summer in front of me to do whatever. Because I have the time, Roxy now gets walked twice a day, which she loves, and which gives me exercise. She loves to visit with other dogs and people along the way. She especially likes to stop by old Mr Carter's house, because he is usually out on his porch, and he always has a doggie bone for her. Roxy loves old Mr Carter. He lives alone, has no family that I know of, and is friendly to everyone who passes by. I think my dad said he was in some war and got hurt. I can't remember the details. We also stop to say hi to Mrs Beck and her toddler Alex when they are out for their walk. Roxy loves little ones and is very gentle when she is around them. It's kind of fun seeing the neighborhood through a dog's eye, as we must stop at certain trees, sniff at all passersby, watch the cars pass, and bark a greeting to all the animals we see. Roxy makes me laugh and always puts me in a good mood. She is good on the leash, and I don't mind walking her, unless it is raining.

"Myka," my mom called, "it's time to get up."

"But there's no school today," I hollered back! "Can't I sleep in? Why do I have to get up so early?"

"Early?" my mom asked. "Mykayla Ava Anderson, it is already ten a.m.! If you want to go to the mall, you had better get a move on!"

"Yikes! Sorry, mom! I'll be down right away!"

We were at Mulberry Hill Mall by eleven. Parking was easy this time of day. We had worked out a strategy for what stores to go to in what order to maximize our time. My mom even said we could go to a restaurant for lunch instead of eating at home, which was a rare treat. Some of my friends at school don't like to clothes shop with their moms because they like such different things, but my mom understands style and is pretty reasonable. I am not too wild, either so we get along pretty well, so far anyway. Besides, she is the one with the credit cards! First priority for this trip were some comfy summer outfits… we would worry about new fall school clothes later. Some of the stores had sales, some not; we found everything we needed in six different places, and I was very happy. We decided to have lunch at Bucky's Diner, because they have the best burgers around and my mom could get her usual salad.

Chapter 2

Over the weekend, just when I was feeling the lowest over Junie's departure, my parents surprised me with a new bike. It is ten-speed to help with Mulberry Hill, and purple with yellow stripes. It is really cool. I celebrated by riding all over town. I did fall off one time, though I didn't tell my parents. I cut the corner at Walnut and Oakton too sharply and the front wheel hit my shoe on the pedal and down I went. No damage to anything, though, as I had my helmet on and the bike just sort of skidded a bit and then went down. I couldn't even see any major scratches on the bike (or on me), so all is good. Even better, I don't think anyone even saw me go down! I wish I had someone to ride with, but my other friends are either away with family like Junie or a couple are at camp already, while some are playing sports and others are swimming or on the local gymnastics team. I never was much interested in sports, am afraid of being on stage since I was little and have little coordination for gymnastics, so I never get involved in those things. So, while all my friends have full summer schedules of practice, I have lots of free time. I did ride to the library and check out one of the books on Mrs Ferguson's list. I figured I should be ready for the next rainy day when I can just stay home and read for a while. That is being productive, isn't it?

Dear Diary,

I've never written in a diary before, but something hugely important happened to me today and I must tell somebody. I surely cannot tell my parents. I met a new friend today. Her name is Parva. She lives in... well, she lives in the woods... I guess is the best description. Technically, she lives between Fisher's Market and Sally's Salon. Weird, I know. That's why I need to write to you about it. I am so happy to have a friend this summer!!!!

***

I was gliding up Mulberry Hill like I have done thousands of times since I was raised here in this town. The bike was riding smoothly, there was a soft breeze, and I was relaxed. For some unknown reason, I happened to look to my right as I first passed Sally's Salon and then Fisher's Market. The buildings are very close to one another, though they do not touch. There is a small strip of land between them, and I mean small. It actually is kind of a hill that if you followed it would lead to back parking lots, but it is so narrow it is pretty useless. I don't even think it is wide enough for my bike to fit now that I think about it. Anyway, like I said, I was pedaling along and happened to look to my right and saw something really shiny between the two buildings. I had never seen it before. It really stood out. What was odd was that it couldn't have been a reflection from the sun because the buildings would have blocked any light. The shiny thing distracted me, and I almost hit a pedestrian crossing the street! I swung back around, and this time looked to my left. The shiny thing was still there. I was positive I would have noticed it another time if it had always been there. What was it? When did it appear? Why was it between the two buildings? Did someone drop something with batteries that emitted a light? Was it a treasure? My mind started racing with the possibilities. No one else walking by seemed to have noticed it or was paying it any attention. I just had to investigate! I parked and locked my bike at Fisher's and walked over to the place between the two buildings. No one was paying any attention to me, as they were busy going about their own business. I scrambled up the hill to see what the shiny thing was. As I reached forward to grab it, I fell into a hole.

***

I felt like the earth had swallowed me up and then spit me out. It was kinda dark and it took a while for my eyes to adjust to the dimness. I was in some kind of forest with very tall trees. It was cool and there was not a lot of sun. It was eerily quiet. I admit I was a little scared, but I was excited, too. What had I discovered in my little town of Hickory Springs? How did I really get here? How long had this forest existed right between Fisher's and Sally's?

Weird. I brushed dirt off my jeans and stood up. There looked to be a kind of path that led off to the right, and I began to walk away. Everywhere I looked, things were lush and green. And it was quiet, very quiet. Maybe too quiet. No noises from the cars on Mulberry Hill, no beeping of the scanner from Fisher's Market, no kids yelling, no animals scurrying about... no anything. I walked deeper into the forest. There were rock formations and then I heard the gurgling of water. I found a stream with crystal-clear water. So clear I could see my reflection in it. Fortunately for me, the water wasn't very deep, and I could see clear down to the bottom. No pollution here. I walked along the path and saw all kinds of flowers, trees and bushes I had never laid eyes on before. Some of them were very vibrant in color, others were different because of their shape. After about twenty minutes of walking, I decided to turn around. I was thinking that I would find my way back to my starting place and figure out how to exit (there was an exit, wasn't there?). If I got in once, I could get in some other time; it could become my special place this summer. Well, that was my plan. But then it was on the way back that I met her.

    She was short, shorter than me. She was dark-skinned and had jet-black hair which was kind of all over the place. Her face looked different than mine, but it is kind of hard to describe. Her nose was bigger and flatter, her forehead sloped back some and it kind of looked like she didn't have a neck. Her arms and legs were thick and strong like tree trunks, kinda hairy and much bigger than my puny appendages. We both just froze and stared. I don't know who was more scared. Then, finally, I realized that I was probably a guest in her world, so I made the first move: I smiled. It was, I admit, a tentative, scared kind of smile and not fully genuine, but it was the only thing I could think of. At first, she did nothing. Then she looked around her – who (or what?) was she looking for? – then tentatively looked back at me and smiled in return. I didn't realize I had been holding my breath. My task of finding my way out temporarily side-tracked, I reached out my hand in a gesture of greeting. She had a puzzled look on her face. Then I had to laugh at myself to think that she would automatically know that shaking hands is a way to greet. So, I sat down right where I was in the packed dirt on the trail and motioned with my hand for her to join me. She did! Though she didn't sit real close to me, she did sit down near me. I touched my chest and said, "Myka." Then I pointed to her with raised eyebrows, hoping she would tell me her name.

"EMK," she repeated. Well, not exactly what my parents had in mind.

I tried again. "Myka," I said, pointing to my chest.

"EMKA," she repeated. We were getting closer. I pointed to her. She pointed to herself and said what sounded to me like "Parva". When I repeated that, she got a big smile on her face, so I figured that was close enough.

"Myka," I said, pointing to me, and then "Parva," pointing to her.

"Parva," she said, pointing to her, and then "EMKA," pointing to me. Well, it would have to do for now.

I was so excited. I had a million questions to ask her. Language was obviously a barrier. And I was getting a little worried about time. Without the sun to guide me, I really didn't know how long I had been inside here. And I still wasn't sure how to get out. So, as much as I hated to do so, I decided I had better head for home, fully confident that if I wanted to, I could figure out a way to come back another day.

Getting out was harder than getting in, because I had to find the right location, and there was no shiny thing to guide me. Luckily, I was born with a pretty good sense of direction – I get that from my dad, definitely not from my mom. After several false tries, I finally found the passageway. I had left Parva on the trail as she went in the other direction when I stood up to leave. She actually seemed a little afraid of going in the direction I was headed, though I have no idea why. Anyway, I found an indentation in the ground, placed my foot on it and tumbled out onto the hill between Fisher's and Sally's. Just like that. It was the weirdest thing. Actually, I was beginning to wonder if it was all a dream, but my bike was there and I noticed it was near dusk and I knew I had to get home in a hurry or I would have some big explaining to do with my parents, which was the LAST thing I wanted to have to do.

Chapter 3

I had strange dreams that night. I kept seeing Parva and trying to make sense of her world. How did it get there? Was it real? Should I tell anybody? Is Parva all alone? Does she need help? I tossed and turned all night as I tried to make sense out of my experience. I sure wish Junie was here. We could be talking about this and going through this together. Is Parva my responsibility now, like Roxy is? I mean, if she is all alone, how does she eat, where does she sleep, how does she spend her day? It must be very lonely. I resolved to go back and visit her in the daylight and to take my watch this time so I could keep better track of the passage of time. It was so hard to do that in that forest. I would be better prepared next time. Should I bring her a little present? Like what? I was overwhelmed with thoughts of her.

After breakfast and after mom left for work, I told dad I was going for a bike ride.

"How do you like your new bike?" he asked.

"I love it! It's perfect!" I explained. "I probably won't be home for lunch."

"Oh? Going out with one of your friends? Do you need some money?" dad asked.

"Hmm. That would probably help. I haven't been babysitting in a while and my funds are low. Thanks, dad. You're the best!"

With two ten-dollar bills safely in my pocket, I grabbed my backpack and light jacket and headed for the door. As I rode to downtown, I kept wondering what I should buy Parva as a treat. I had already decided I would bring her food. Should I buy something healthy like chicken or a salad, or something fun like candy? I parked my bike and checked briefly to make sure the shiny spot between the two buildings was still there before I bought the food. But I didn't see it! I carefully climbed up the hill and kind of stomped all around, but nothing happened. Did I imagine the whole thing? I know I had the right place, but it clearly wasn't here right now. I was confused. What should I do now? Since it was still early, I decided to use my time to investigate the whole situation more thoroughly at the library.

Mr Scott, the reference librarian, was sitting at his desk working at the computer. I went up to him and after he looked up, I asked, "What do you call a place in the ground that collapses right under you?"

He thought for a minute and then said, "Are you thinking of a sink hole?"

"What is that?"

"It is when part of the ground gives way, revealing the structure underneath. Whatever was on top of the sink hole collapses, is often destroyed, and made unusable."

"What is under a sink hole?" I asked.

"Whatever was holding up the above-ground structure. For example, if the sink hole happened on a street, you would see the street foundation underneath. If it happened over a house, you would see the house foundation."

"Could the sink hole cover itself back up again? I mean, reverse itself so you didn't know it was there? Like going through something but then everything being back to normal?"

"No."

"Do you know of anything that would?"

Mr Scott pondered the question a bit. "If you're asking about going from one place to another without a trace, you might be thinking of something in science fiction. There are things called transporters and portals that do that, but they're not real."

I took out my notebook and wrote down the word 'transporter' and the word 'portal'. I wanted to look those two words up in the dictionary. I thanked Mr Scott and found the huge library dictionary. This dictionary is so large and heavy it would never fit in someone's backpack. After reading both definitions, I decided that 'portal' was the best word to use for what I had discovered. That still didn't answer my question of why the portal was there yesterday but not there today, nor did it solve the riddle of who Parva was or where she came from. Then I remembered something I had seen on TV, and I had an idea.

"Mr Scott, who were the people before me?"

Raising his eyebrows, Mr Scott said, "You mean like your grandparents?"

I shook my head. "No, before them."

"You mean from another country?"

"I don't know," I said honestly. "I mean, like way before me. Like in the beginning. Maybe they didn't even look exactly like me."

Standing up, Mr Scott said, "Follow me." We walked over to the reference section, and he pulled down a big book and showed me a diagram of a fish that over time turns into a human like me. It was simply amazing.

"Is this what you mean?"

"Yes!" I shouted, even though I was in the library. "This is exactly what I mean! Thank you, Mr Scott! Now, can you show me where this section is in the library?"

When he pointed out the section, it took all my will power not to run – I was in a library, after all.

***

There was Parva. Or at least a reasonable picture of her right there on that page in the book under 'Cro-Magnon'. I could hardly believe it. How could she be alive? She was my ancestor from long, long, long ago. None of them were supposed to be alive any more. And how did that forest get to be there? Does she spend all day in the forest? Is she all alone? What does she eat? Where does she sleep? Is it scary? Some of the books in the Cro-Magnon section were adult books and hard for me to read. I looked through many of them and read what I could. Then I realized my stomach was growling and I looked at my watch. Lunchtime already! Where had the morning gone? I checked out a few of the books and headed back downtown. I wanted to check for the portal one more time before I gave up. I locked my bike and walked between the two buildings. There was something shining between them again. It was the portal! Unbelievable! I decided it must depend on the time of day! Why didn't I think of that earlier? I went into Fisher's Market and looked around. I bought some barbecue boneless chicken wings, two cans of Sprite, some mashed potatoes and gravy, some Oreos, and a package of Twizzlers. Armed with extra napkins, everything went into my backpack, and I headed toward the portal.

I slipped in and let my eyes adjust to the low light. Everything was as it had been the day before. I got on the path and turned to the right. The forest was so big. How would I find her? I began to walk, looking left and right as I went. After about ten minutes, I heard a tree branch rustle. I stopped and listened. "Parva?" I called. No answer. I walked a few more steps and out of the brush she stepped. I was so relieved to see her! I sat down on the trail and motioned her over. She first looked around, then joined me. She was smiling. I slowly and deliberately unzipped my backpack. I didn't want her to be afraid. I took out the napkins and laid them out on the dirt of the trail. Then I put a barbecue wing on each napkin, laid out the little containers of mashed potatoes and gravy with the spork, and opened the Sprite cans. She watched me with much curiosity. I picked up my wing and took a bite. I chewed carefully, said "yum" and rubbed my tummy. I tried to invite her to do the same. She cocked her head in concentration as she watched me take another bite. She must have smelled the chicken (one of my favorites) and she moved closer to me. Imagine my delight when she took her first bite! But oh, what a face she made! I thought she was going to spit it out. I took a drink from the can and invited her to do the same. I didn't think about the first time I ever had a carbonated drink and how the bubbles first feel... she started to giggle and then she burped! Her giggling made me laugh! Soon, we were enjoying our lunch – she much more tentatively than I – and laughing in between. She kept holding the food out in front of her and smelling it first before she took a bite. The spork was way too hard for her to manage, so we both ate the mashed potatoes with our fingers. Yeah, it was messy, but we made it work. When I handed her the Oreo, I showed her how to take it apart and eat half of it at a time. I really wish I had a glass of cold milk to give her along with it, but I didn't, so we had to make do. She choked a little on the Twizzler and I tried to show her that she had to chew it up more than what she was doing. You can't just put it in your mouth and swallow those things.

After we were done eating, I cleaned everything up and put it all back in my backpack. I did put several cookies and Twizzlers into a little baggie for her to take with her after I was gone as a little present. She seemed reluctant to take it at first, but finally did. I checked my watch. Because of the late availability of the portal and our visit, I didn't have much time left to get home before my mom. I told Parva I would come again tomorrow and that she should look for me. I used a combination of words and hand gestures, but I don't really know how much she understood. I really wanted to hug her goodbye but wasn't sure she would be okay with that. I reached out both my hands and took hers and smiled, then I did it. I hugged her ever so gently. Her clothes felt rough and scratchy. She did not hug me back, but just stood there. But she did not pull away, either. She looked kind of sad when I turned to leave, but she did not follow me. I slipped through the portal and made it home in plenty of time. What an amazing day.

  As it turned out, I couldn't go into town the next day. My dad had me working all day in the garage. The one good thing that came out of it (besides a clean garage) was that we found my old wagon. I had been thinking about Parva all day and thinking that there might be some things I should take her. I wondered how I would carry all the things to her, but when we found my old wagon, I began to wonder if it would go through the portal or not. But what kind of things did she need? Blankets? Pillows? Food? Clothes? Toys? I realized I needed more information. I would have to see what she had to determine what she still needed. The other thing I began to worry about was my parents. Do I tell them what I discovered? They are both pretty level-headed and don't get upset easily, but they may want to call the police or something, and that would ruin everything. I mean, I don't think Parva is in any kind of trouble that the police need to be involved, no danger of any kind that I could see. She's just my friend. At what point do I let my parents in on my secret? I will have to think on that one for a while.

Chapter 4

Dear Diary,

I am bummed because I couldn't go to town today. All I can think about is Parva. I counted the money I have been saving and it comes to $35.67. While that may seem like a lot, it is not going to buy a lot for her. I know because when my mom and I went to the mall to buy me some new summer clothes, she spent more than that and we only bought a few outfits. How can I buy her clothes and food and bed stuff and everything else on $35? I am going to have to get my parents involved, I think. But what is the best way to do that? Timing is everything.

"Mom, can I talk to you?" I asked one morning after breakfast.

"Sure, sweetheart. What's up?"

"I need some advice. Let's pretend you have a friend who doesn't have a lot. You want to help her have some things she might need, but you only have a little bit of money from babysitting. Even if you use all the money you saved, it would probably not be enough to help her. What would you do?"

"Well, I guess if it was a friend of mine who really needed the stuff – not just wanted the stuff – but needed the stuff, I would try to find a way to get extra money to help her in whatever way I could."

"How would you go about doing that?" I asked.

"Well, you could try to earn extra money by doing extra jobs, you could ask for money from people who have extra, and you could have, like, a bake sale or something. Do you know someone in need?"

"Yes, but not very well. I just met her, and she is kind of shy."

"Why don't you bring her here so we can meet her and try to figure out how to help her?"

"Um... I don't think that would work too well. Maybe later. Thanks for helping me think this through, though," I said, as I started to leave.

"Myka, wait," my mom replied. "Here's $20 to help you get started with your 'project'. Let me know how it goes."

"Gee, thanks, mom!"

***

I put a butter knife, a roll of paper towels, a loaf of bread, a jar of peanut butter and one of jelly, two bottles of water, a pillow, a sleeping bag, and a pair of flannel pajamas into a big garbage bag and placed it on the wagon. At the last minute, I threw in one of my teddy bears. Because of the wagon, I would have to walk to town rather than ride my bike, which I wasn't exactly looking forward to. I wondered again whether I would be able to get the wagon through the portal or not, but I knew I had to try. An hour later, I was finally there, though a little out of breath from Mulberry Hill. The portal wasn't there yet as it was only eleven thirty a.m. I figured I had to wait about thirty minutes or so. I leaned up against a tree and tried to imagine what it would be like giving Parva all these things. I knew the pajamas would be too big, but they would be soft and warm. I kind of went into a daydream because I suddenly woke with a start when a truck backfired on the street in front of me and startled me back to reality. I looked at my watch. 12.10. Show time.

The portal was there waiting for me. It was a little bit of a challenge pushing the wagon up the hill, especially since I didn't really want to draw attention to myself. I stopped just before the portal to make sure no one was looking, then took that next step – and wagon and all, we dropped in. The wagon actually tipped on the other side, but the garbage bag kept everything from falling all over the place. I started down the path and this time I hadn't gone very far when Parva came right out onto the path to greet me. I walked up to her and gave her a big hug! Then she saw the wagon and her eyes got real big. But before I could start emptying it out to show her, she was gesturing to me to follow her. So, we walked about thirty minutes, me looking at all the newness around me, her looking over her shoulder at me pulling the wagon. What a sight we must have been! We walked further than I had gone that first day, but still on the trail. I was glad Parva was leading me. The landscape started changing to more rocky structures with caves. As we turned a bend, it was my turn for my eyes to grow big. There in front of me was an enormous cave, and standing in front of it was a bigger version of Parva with a baby, and off in the back was a great big male version of Parva! I was shocked to the core! She wasn't alone! Was this her family? Parva was shyly smiling at my disbelief. The others were staring at me warily. I managed to smile and tried to look friendly. After what seemed like an eternity of staring at me, the mom and baby went back into the cave and the dad went about his business. With relief, I guessed I had passed inspection.

Parva sat down on the ground, and I sat next to her. I took out the loaf of bread and the peanut butter and jelly. I made a sandwich and cut it in half. I started to eat and encouraged Parva to do the same. She trusted me and took a bite after first smelling it. She made a funny face, but then smiled. She kind of made a sucking sound and I realized the peanut butter was sticking in her mouth. I opened a bottle of water for her and held it out to her. I showed her how to take a drink, but some of it dribbled down her chin. The water was cold, and she gasped. Then her mom said, "Parva!"

She immediately stood up and went to her, carrying the sandwich. She held it out to her mom. Her mom smelled it, pulled apart the two pieces of bread and looked at it. She touched the peanut butter with her finger and found it sticky. She put her finger in her mouth and her face got the funniest look on it, but I didn't dare laugh out loud. She put the two pieces back together and took a bite just as Parva had done. After a time, she nodded 'yes' and gave the sandwich back to Parva, who came back to join me. Whew! Another test that was passed!

    I showed Parva the pillow and sleeping bag and demonstrated how to use them. She watched me with great attention. I showed her the pajamas and put them on over my clothes, and that made her laugh because there were penguins on them. When she touched them, I could tell she liked the soft feel of them, because she held them up close to her body. Soon, her mom came down to investigate the gifts. I was afraid she wasn't going to allow Parva to keep them. I didn't bring some for everyone because I didn't know there was anyone else besides Parva living in the forest. I would be better prepared next time! I made her mom her own sandwich and one for her dad as well. It was a big hit! I was feeling pretty good about myself right about now. I wondered what the baby ate, because I don't know too much about little babies in either world. Parva looked so happy to have me there and so proud to have me as a friend. We finished eating, played with the teddy bear, did some exploring, got to know each other better and learned to communicate better. Just as I was thinking it was about time for me to head out, around the corner of the path came two big male Parvas (brothers?) carrying a dead animal between them. It sort of looked like some kind of antelope, but it was upside down and gutted, so it was kind of hard to tell. They were not happy to see me, and I quickly got myself and my wagon out of their way. This seemed like a good time to say goodbye, so I motioned to Parva that I had to go back on the trail, and would she take me back? It was a long walk back to the portal, and as always, Parva said goodbye to me before I made that last turn to reach the portal, showing a lot of reluctance to go any further. The wagon was a lot easier now to maneuver since it was empty, and I got home faster than the trip into town had been.

I couldn't stop thinking about Parva's family. That sure was a surprise. They seemed to accept me okay. Parva must have told her mom about me before I met her, because she seemed less shocked than I was. I didn't really hear them talk to each other, but they must communicate. I started to plan what I would bring the next time I went. I needed more sleeping bags and pillows for sure.

The next few days involved taking supplies to Parva. They started to expect me now, and even her brothers seemed less distant, especially when they got their own sleeping bags. One thing my dad and I discovered when we cleaned out the garage was the pile of camping stuff, they had bought a long time ago. Before I was born and then when I was a baby, my mom and dad used to go camping in the National Park. There were quite a few cooking utensils for cooking over an open fire, a tent and some plates and dishes. Since my parents got their current jobs and I got older, we stopped camping. My guess is they would never miss that stuff. So, I took all of it to Parva's family. I showed Parva's mom how to boil water with the cooking pot over the open campfire, because I also brought them spaghetti! I walked through Fisher's and picked out a ton of stuff to bring them: spaghetti and sauce, mac and cheese (using powdered milk), canned peaches (using a handheld can opener), beans, corn, beets, lettuce, cheese, ramen noodles, soup, canned pasta, tuna fish, sardines, tomatoes, cream cheese, celery, mushrooms, onions, pickles, Sprite, Pepsi, bottled water, juice, granola bar, cereal, donuts, muffins, cake, chocolate candy bars, apple sauce, bananas, apples, oranges, potatoes, potato chips and dip, tortilla chips and salsa, rice bags and chili. I brought them a wide variety of things at first so they could tell me what they liked best. Their most favorite from that list was the spaghetti and sauce, ramen noodles and the donuts. But their most favorite overall, and the thing they couldn't seem to get enough of, was peanut butter and jelly sandwiches. My kind of family!

Chapter 5

My family and I went to church on Sunday, followed by going out to lunch, so I couldn't visit Parva. I missed seeing her, but I knew she had enough food to last a while as I had been bringing stuff to her family all week. Besides, my funds were depleted, and I needed to regroup. Then for three days it rained, and I couldn't get into town. I did read one book from Mrs Ferguson's list, though, with Roxy cuddled up in my lap. I will have to go to the library to get another title as I have just about finished this first one. I wonder if Junie has even started one yet.

Thursday morning the sun finally came out. It was going to be a beautiful day. I asked my dad for an advance on my allowance before I headed into town with the wagon. He kind of raised his eyebrows since I asked early last time, too, but he didn't complain. After walking Roxy, I took an empty garbage bag and put it in the wagon and headed for town. I must have walked faster than usual or left a little earlier, because I got to town pretty quickly and had plenty of time to go to Fisher's and get to the portal as soon as it was available. Since it had been a while since I last saw them, I figured their food supply was probably running a little low, but so was my bank account... it was a lot of responsibility! I felt some stress over the situation, which I didn't expect, especially since this was supposed to be my summer vacation. At the top of Mulberry Hill, I stopped and sat in the wagon to rest and to count my money. My back was to the portal because I had to go to Fisher's first, so I was concentrating on that.

"EMKA?" I heard a tiny voice say.

I almost thought I didn't hear anything. I sat very still, not moving in the wagon. "EMKA?" the tiny voice said again.

I whipped around and, oh my gosh, there was Parva standing in my world. My heart just stopped. I stared, dumbfounded. "UNGR" she said, which is her word for 'hungry'. Did she come through the portal to tell me she needed food? Oh, why did I not visit her the past few days? What kind of friend am I anyway? I ran to her and gave her a big hug. Her eyes were as big as saucers as she looked out onto my world; she kept blinking her eyes because of the bright sun. Worried that she would draw unnecessary attention to herself, I told her to lay down on the hill and that I would be right back. I dashed into Fisher's, grabbed some bread, peanut and jelly and a single sheet. After waiting for what seemed like forever in the checkout lane, I ran back out and wrapped the sheet around her. I thought that would be less obvious than her animal clothes. I made her a quick sandwich to ward off her hunger, and then we had to strategize. Now that she was 'out', what did she want to do?

"EMKA OM," she said. She wanted me to take her to my home! What would my parents say? What would her parents say? Did they even know she was missing? So many questions were swirling around inside my head.

"Are you sure it is okay with your mom?" I asked her. "Your mom, does she know?"

"MEMA YES," she replied.

Now I got excited! Parva was going to go home with me! Think of all the things we could do! Wait till I tell Junie! There were probably going to be some bumps in the road, but once my parents knew about her and I didn't have to deal with all of this alone any more, that will be a grand thing. Oh, this is working out quite well. As long as she doesn't miss her family too much... it will be like a little vacation for her! A vacation in the modern world, and I can show her everything. Oh, this is going to be wonderful – and I started laughing. Parva didn't know what I was laughing at, but with her stomach now full, she joined in with me. It did draw some looks from the passersby, but I didn't care. I picked up the arm of the wagon and we started walking home. I offered to let her ride in the wagon, but she was just as content to walk by my side. Everything we passed was new to her... and bright... and loud. She had a lot of things to get used to in this crazy modern world!

***

When we got home, my mom's car was not in the garage and dad was working in the study. I got Parva up to my room without incident. I wanted to introduce her to my parents together, not one at a time. I showed Parva my bed, and when she sat down and felt its softness, she was shocked. I showed her my closet full of clothes, which, unfortunately, were all too big for her. She saw my stuffed animal collection, my computer, and my desk full of 'stuff'. My room is painted in a soft yellow, and she even gently touched the walls to feel the color. But the biggest shock of all to her was when she looked in the mirror. I have never seen a funnier expression on a person's face. She just did not know what to make of it. Then, when I went to stand behind her so she could see both of us in the mirror, she was very confused at first. She tentatively reached out to touch the glass. I tried to explain what the mirror was and what it was used for. She just stared at me through the mirror, and I could tell she was trying to process the information. It was kind of funny, but I didn't dare laugh because she was being so serious about it. I drew her attention over to my window, which looks out on our back yard. Roxy was out there romping about, and I told her that was my pet dog. I tried to explain that this is the cave I live in, and that she can stay here with me for a while. I told her I have parents, too, but no brothers or sisters like she has. Then I heard my mom's car pull into the garage. I would know pretty soon whether Parva could stay with us or not. I was starting to get nervous. As my mom came in, she let Roxy in, who came bounding up the stairs into my room. Roxy stopped on a dime when she saw Parva and just froze. Parva froze, too, a little afraid. I went over and picked up Roxy and started petting her. She started licking my face. Parva broke into a wide grin. Then Parva came over and Roxy sniffed her. The dog was more interested in her clothes made from animals than in Parva herself. But soon they were fast friends, and I had them both sit on the bed, and I left them playing with each other while I went down to deal with my parents.

"Hi, Myka, how was your day?" my mom asked, as she placed the groceries on the table.

"Good," I replied. "Was your day a busy one?"

"Oh, we had a crying child in the office today," my mom said. "It took quite a bit to get her calmed down. Where's your dad?"

"I think he is in the study," I told her. "Um, I really need to talk to the two of you."

"Okay, honey. We'll make some time after dinner to have some family time."

"No, that's not going to work," I said sheepishly. "I kind of need to talk to both of you now, before dinner."

"Are you in trouble, Myka?" my mom asked, looking worried.

"No, but please, mom, it can't wait. Can I go call dad?"

"Sure. I'll get these groceries put away while you go get him and I'll make us all some tea."

"What's on your mind?" my dad asked.

"Well, you may not really believe me, but I have been trying to help a friend…"

"Your father and I know you have been asking for extra money. We hoped it was for a good reason," mom said.

"And today that friend came home with me!"

"That's wonderful!" exclaimed my mom. "We would love to meet her. I don't know why you look so worried, Myka. You know we would support you. You have a good heart. We can help her family, too, if that is what you are going to ask next."

"Not exactly," I said. "You see, she is not from our world." At that, my parents looked at each other with very confused looks.

"I guess," my mom started to say, "we don't really understand…"

"No, you wouldn't," I said, "because it is all very strange to me, too; but please, you must believe me. I don't know who else to turn to."

My dad said, "Why don't you start at the beginning?"

I said, "Let me bring her down and then I will tell her story. Is that okay?"

My parents just stared at Parva. I could tell they were in shock. We moved to the living room, where it was more comfortable, and it helped that Roxy chose to jump in Parva's lap and settle herself there. I told my parents all about the portal. I told them about meeting Parva first, then meeting her family, then trying to feed them all, and then how I couldn't visit for a while, and how Parva got hungry and came out of the portal all on her own. With each explanation, my parents grew more uncertain; I could tell by their body language and the looks they kept giving each other.

"Take me to this portal now, Myka," my dad said in his best principal voice.

"I can't," I replied. "The portal is open only during certain times of the day. It is too late in the day right now. I could take you tomorrow at noon, though."

Breathing out a long breath, my father said, "Okay, let's plan on doing that. In the meantime, for tonight only, our friend can stay with us. But I want to talk to her parents to see what they think about all this."

"Um, dad," I gently said, "her parents don't speak English."

"Oh, um, yes, of course, I wasn't thinking about that. Well, somehow, I need to ask them about their daughter and what they want to do. I imagine our world is a little different to theirs. They may not want her being influenced by our world."

"I'm proud of you, Myka," my mom said. "You did a very brave thing." Then she smiled at Parva.

Parva shyly smiled back. I breathed a sigh of relief. If I could get at least one of my parents on my side, it would be so much easier!

"I need to get dinner ready. Why don't you girls help set the table and then get washed up? We will be eating soon," said mom.

***

My parents didn't seem to mind that Parva ate with her fingers. There would be time enough later if she stayed with us to teach her how to use a spoon, fork and knife. With it all being so new, you couldn't expect everything to go perfectly. We didn't know how old Parva was, but she was physically smaller than me, and, of course, built a little differently. Both my parents agreed that she would probably be uncomfortable staying in the guest bedroom by herself, especially on her first night, so it was agreed that she would sleep in my bedroom with me. It was almost like having an instant sister! I was so excited. But my mom worried about what she called 'hygiene'. My mom decided that before bedtime, Parva would have to have her first bath and get that crazy hair of hers washed. My mom didn't want her in bed with me without being clean. I didn't know how Parva would take to being washed up, but I tried to prepare her for it. Actually, it was my idea that I take a bath first and let Parva watch, so she could see what it was like. I'm way too old for my mom to give me baths now, but for this one time, my mom, Parva and I all got into the bathroom and made a show of taking a bath and getting my hair washed. I made lots of pleasing sound effects and played some in the water to show her it could be fun. Then I got out and put on soft jammies (that fit me) and we emptied the bathtub water and encouraged Parva to get in. It worked! As long as I stayed in there with her, she was willing to let my mom first wash her and then her unruly hair. Actually, my mom had to put clean water in the tub three different times, so much dirt came off her. Wow! We got her dried off and put on soft jammies (that didn't fit her), and then we went into my bedroom and hopped into clean sheets, with Roxy right there. We both smelled so good. Mom didn't really know what to do with Parva's clothes. It wasn't like you could throw them into the washing machine. So, she got a garbage bag and a box and wrapped them up and put them in my closet for when we needed them again.

Parva was awake long before the sun was up. I had a sense someone was watching me – you know that creepy feeling you get – and when I opened my eyes, she was staring at me. I told her to go back to sleep because it was way too early. I rubbed her back and she fell back asleep. Unfortunately, I didn't, because I started worrying about going back through the portal with my dad. How would I find her family on my own? Parva didn't want to go back. Would dad fit through the portal? I figured if a wagon would, he would, but how would we communicate? So many thoughts racing through my head, and Parva's gentle breathing next to me reminded me that I had gotten myself into this situation and that somehow, I would see it through to the end.

Apparently, my parents talked after we went to bed last night. My mom told my dad about the bath water and about the need for different-sized clothes. My dad was concerned about how we were going to explain Parva's presence. They told us at breakfast, if people asked, Parva was a cousin visiting from Australia and not used to American ways. I had to go look Australia up on the map. I think they were thinking Australian aborigine because of her physical features, but most people wouldn't get past the Australia idea. Why that would be a cousin of ours is beyond me, but Parva was a kind of cousin from long ago – a very long time ago to be sure – but a cousin, nonetheless. So, it worked. Parva would have to get used to people staring at her. She had never been in a car before, never seen an airplane, never been on a bike, never seen water come out of a faucet, never been in a soft bed, never seen a pet dog, never been to a store, never seen lots of people in one place... the list just goes on and on and on. Everything was new to her! And I mean everything!

Fortunately, when my parents bought me my new bike, we didn't get rid of my old one, so I intended to try to teach her how to ride! I couldn't wait until Junie came home! What a surprise all this would be for her. But first things first. Parva needed something to wear that fit her. My clothes were too big.

That morning after breakfast, my mom went to the mall. She didn't take Parva with her because she had nothing to wear that fit. My mom picked out several different outfits in different sizes, not knowing for sure which ones would work out best. She planned to return the sizes that didn't fit. While she was gone, my dad and I were showing different things to Parva in books, and he even took Parva for a ride in the car around the neighborhood. Both of us were trying our best to give English words to things in Parva's new world. She almost never spoke, but she seemed to be absorbing what we told her. My dad's teacher background came in very handy. We all met back at the house late morning and my mom, and I helped Parva try on the clothes. Nothing was perfect, but we got pretty close to a size that fit. We had an early lunch and then my dad announced that we were going to the portal. My stomach twisted in a knot; I was so nervous.

Chapter 6

Dad and I drove to the portal. We were both nervous, though I think for different reasons. After parking the car, he told me that he wanted to get clarification from Parva's parents that it was all right for her to be 'out' with us. He also wanted to know how long she could visit us, and what, if anything, they needed. I was worried about first finding her family by ourselves, and then HOW my dad was going to communicate with them. Everything was so complicated. I showed dad the shining portal, and he casually looked around to see who might be watching us. People were scurrying about, minding their own business, so he said, "Let's go!" and I took his hand, and we went through. He was stunned. "Where are we?" he whispered to me.

"We are in Parva's world," I whispered back. I am not sure why we felt the need to whisper.

"Which way do we go?" he asked.

"Follow me," I said, more optimistically than I felt.

We took the path to the right and began to walk. Dad asked if it was dangerous being in here. I said I had never seen any live animals or anything that made me afraid. "Actually," I admitted, "the scariest thing is the silence."

We held hands as we walked, and I could tell my dad was really nervous, because his hand was sweating even though it wasn't hot in the forest. "Do you know what you're going to say?" I asked.

"Yes," he said. "I have it all prepared." That's just like my dad... he is a principal, after all, and talks to different kinds of people all the time.

It was so beautiful in the forest. Trees, flowers, bushes of all kinds and colors. There were things neither one of us had ever seen before, especially the vibrant colors and the cleanliness of the environment. It was beautiful, but oh, so quiet. Suddenly, quite unexpectedly, my dad stopped walking. We still had about ten minutes to go by my calculation. In the middle of the trail, he just stopped, closed his eyes, and took a deep breath. I looked up, alarmed, and thought maybe he was getting sick. After what seemed like forever, he turned to me and said, "We're going home!"

My jaw dropped. "What?" I whispered. "What do you mean? We're going home now before we talk to her parents. But we're almost there!"

He looked at me in a gentle sort of way. "Myka, I wouldn't be able to communicate what I want to say, anyway. Parva seems happy being with us for the time being. She came to us; we did not drag her out. Her parents must know. She can stay as long as she wants to. Let's go home."

At dinner that night, I kept looking at my dad to see if he showed any signs of illness. It just wasn't like him to not follow through on a mission, as he calls his tasks. At the table, he was joking and laughing and talking to Parva and all of us as if nothing weird had happened. Parva wanted words for everything. She wasn't very good at saying the words, but she wanted to hear what the word was. While we were at the portal, Parva and my mom had started to label things in the house. The door had a label, as did the chair, a book, the garbage can, the refrigerator and the rug. Other things were labeled as well. This was supposed to help her see that letters put together made words, and that is how we communicate, or something like that. After dishes were done, Parva and I took Roxy for a long walk. We went by Juba Park, and Parva watched some little kids on the swings. I thought maybe tomorrow we could go there to play without Roxy, and Parva could try the swings and slide. I really don't know if she would like that movement or not. I did as a kid, but I know not everyone does. After we got home, mom wanted us to take a bath again before we went to bed. It was a lot easier this second time, and mom didn't have to help us, except when it came to Parva's hair. That girl sure has a lot of hair! She keeps touching my shorter, straighter hair, just as I like to touch her wild, longer hair. We are so different from each other, and yet we have things in common, too. It's so weird. I know Junie would like Parva.

    I slept late the next morning. When I woke up, Parva was already out of bed. I panicked a little because I didn't know where she was, but I figured my mom or dad were taking care of her. Imagine my surprise when I walked down the stairs, only to run into a new Parva! My mom had given her a make-over! Her hair was a little shorter and it was combed differently, and she looked very cute. Parva was obviously pleased, as she greeted me with a huge grin!

"Parva!" I cried. "You look wonderful! That has got to be cooler for you in this summer heat!"

"NEW ANMTS," said Parva.

"Yes," I replied. "You have on your new pants as well! Very nice! Let's have some breakfast!"

It was just the three of us for breakfast, as dad was in his study working. Mom turned to me and said, "Myka, I need to ask you something."

"Sure," I replied.

"What really happened when you and your father went through the portal?"

"Um, I am not sure I understand what you are asking," I said.

"Well, he is different since coming back. Before, he was all eager to get Parva back home. Now he is saying that she should stay as long as she wants. I know he didn't talk to her parents, so I wondered what changed his mind."

"I don't really know," I honestly answered. "We were getting close to their cave and all of a sudden he stopped and said that we were going home."

"Were you arguing with him, Myka?"

"No! In fact, we were talking about how beautiful her world was. It was as sudden to me as it probably seemed to you when he told you about it."

"Well, I think we should take her back soon. This exposure can't be good for her."

"I don't think she wants to go home, mom. At least not yet. Can't I show her things around town and help her learn English a little better?"

"Well, your father would certainly agree with you, but I will have to think about it some more. I am growing increasingly uncomfortable having her here. I don't want her hurt in the long run. What are your plans today?"

"I want to take her to Juba Park so she can play on the swings and slide."

"I must work today. Why don't you get your father to take the two of you out to lunch? That would be fun! Maybe on the way home you can drive through Charleston Forest Preserve and let her see what one of our forests looks like. I'll mention it to your dad."

"Thanks. Have a good day at work. Love ya, mom!"

"Love you, too, sweetie."

After chores were finally done, we walked into the beautiful sunshine day to Juba Park. I asked Parva if she wanted to try the slide or the swings first. She decided on the slide, so I showed her on the smaller slide how to climb the ladder, sit down, push off and let go. Her eyes got real big. She had a little difficulty with the rungs of the ladder because she had never done it before and she seemed to be a little afraid of heights, but she closed her eyes and let go and screamed on her way down. She was grinning at the end, even though she landed on her bottom, and was eager to try it again. After several slides, I felt confident she was ready for the big ladder. Again, I went first to show her how. She screamed even louder but laughed at the same time. She loved it. I got bored with the slide much sooner than she did. She went twice as many times as I did. I finally drew her away so she could try the swings. I tried to tell her how very important it was to always hang on. We started off slowly. She was really uncertain as I gently pushed her swing. She started to take her hand off the chain and I yelled at her, which frightened her, but from then on, she held on with both hands. I taught her how to pump with her legs and was only partially successful. She liked the swings, but the slides were definitely her favorite. We tried the monkey bars, and she was much stronger than I was. Actually, it was kinda embarrassing. She went straight across on her first attempt. She was also very good at the small climbing wall they had there. I watched her sense of balance and began to think that maybe, just maybe, I would be able to teach her how to ride a bike. We walked to the corner gas station and got a drink and sat at the park after our exercise and just relaxed. It was so nice to have a friend.

Dad took us out to lunch and then drove us through the nature preserve as mom suggested. She said it was 'MGO', which meant she thought it was good. Unbeknownst to me, dad packed fishing equipment, so we unpacked everything at Connor Lake, put worms on our hooks (well, actually dad did that part) and threw our bobbers into the water. Can you believe Parva caught the first fish? Dad had to help her because she was really confused, but boy was she excited, especially when we made such a big deal about it. It was a nice size blue gill. She picked up the flopping fish and put it to her face to feel it. Then dad put it on a stringer. We all had good luck that afternoon and caught enough for a good fish dinner that night. Parva was fascinated with the whole cleaning to pan to eating process.

Mom wanted to talk to me after supper (uh-oh), and so dad took Parva into the living room to look at some books and continue to build her vocabulary. This is something they had been doing a little bit each day, and it also strengthened the bond between them. Sometimes they looked at my old children's books, and sometimes they looked at adult books. Parva wanted words for everything, and my dad was patient enough to give them to her.

While Parva and dad were occupied, mom made us some tea in the kitchen. "Myka, I've been thinking about something, and I want to know what you think about this idea."

"Okay," I said tentatively. "Are you going to send Parva back home?"

"No. Your father doesn't think that is a good idea for now. This is something quite different. I will need your cooperation, though."

I had a hard time looking my mom in the eye. This didn't sound good. Especially if she wanted to talk to me alone. "Okay," I finally said. "What is it?"

"I want to take Parva to the office and clean her teeth," my mom explained.

"What does that have to do with me?" I asked warily.

"Well, it will be a brand-new experience for her, and there are lots of machines and equipment, and I thought maybe we should do it like we did Parva's first bath."

"But, mom," I protested, "I HATE going to the dentist! You know that! I am terrible in there! I HATE getting my teeth cleaned!"

"I know," mom said softly. "But could you do it for Parva? Just this once? Pretend it wasn't so bad so she wouldn't be scared?"

I sighed deeply. "Let me think about it."

Chapter 7

Dear Diary,

Disaster. My mom has asked me to go to her office to get my teeth cleaned and to have an audience. I always squirm and cry when I get my teeth cleaned because I hate it so much. Sometimes they must give me medicine just so I can get through it, and now I am somehow supposed to be a role model for Parva?? I can't do it. I am not that strong. She is just going to have to go alone. Forget it. Friends can't do everything. If Junie was here, she could go because she doesn't mind the dentist. A bath is one thing... teeth cleaning is something different. NO!! I WILL NOT DO IT!!

The next week was spent with me trying to teach Parva how to ride my old bike. She did have a really good sense of balance, but most of her body strength was in her upper body, so we had to work on getting coordination in her legs and arms for braking. After a couple of days in our driveway and in front of our house, we ventured a little further out, and soon she was riding pretty consistently, much to the delight of both of us. We began to ride all around town, and my dad bought an extra lock in case there were places we wanted to stop at. I finally got up the nerve to take her to the local library. I wanted to show her the book Mr Scott had showed me that had someone like her in it. She stared at it for a long time, just like I had. Maybe she was remembering back to what she looked like in the mirror. There are a gazzilion books in the library, way more than what my father has at home, and she was overwhelmed with that as well. We even checked out some children's books that had a lot of pictures in them.

We rode past my school, and I tried to explain to her that I spend a lot of time in there; but the building was locked, so I couldn't take her inside. We rode past the high school, and I told her that is where my dad works. I did not show her where my mom worked. We had a blast just riding around to different places, racing and seeing new things. Sometimes we brought a picnic lunch, other times we went home for lunch, and sometimes dad took us out. That week flew by.

"It's time, Myka."

"Time for what?" I asked innocently.

"Tomorrow is my day off and you and Parva are going to the office in the afternoon with me to get your teeth cleaned."

"Aww, mom! Do I have to?"

"Yes. It's time for your check-up anyway. Might as well get it over with and help your friend in the process."

I had trouble sleeping that night. Oddly, it was Parva who tried to help by rubbing my back! I didn't see how I could get out of this. Could I – would I – do it for a friend?

That morning after breakfast, my dad surprised us by agreeing to take us to the local pool. I didn't know if Parva could swim or not. He was going to go with us as an extra safety measure. We piled into the car with all our towels and swimming stuff, and Parva didn't know what to expect. Though the sun was shining, it wasn't the hottest day of the month, so the pool was only moderately crowded, which was good. We started out in the kiddie pool, which I tired of very quickly, but was the right place for Parva to practice. She thought it was so neat that people actually got in the water. She thought the water was cold at first, but then she got used to the temperature. My dad agreed to stay with her if I wanted to go to the regular pool to swim, which I did. I needed to burn off my anxiety for what was going to happen that afternoon at my mom's office. My dad tried to get Parva to put her face under water by holding her breath, but she was too afraid. But she had a blast splashing water, floating and kicking when my dad held her up. She was top-heavy, so she floated kind of weird, but she managed. She also enjoyed wrapping up in a soft towel after she got out and rubbing her hair dry. She was grinning ear to ear from the experience, and even though there is water in her world, it appears she never went into it before. After we were dried and changed, dad took us out to lunch at a place that has an aquarium theme. I had never been there before. Fish tanks lined the perimeter of the restaurant, and they had tropical fish of all kinds. It was astounding! It was very relaxing to eat and watch the fish swim at the same time. At one point, Parva reached into a tank to grab a fish and my dad stopped her just in time. He had to explain to her that these are not fish we eat, just watch. Parva was almost too excited to eat, though. Never before had she seen fish so little and of so many different colors, and she was just simply astounded! Dad spent time explaining to her where fish live, how they move and breathe and that when we went fishing earlier, those were fish, too, but a different kind that you couldn't see. Parva just seems to be a sponge and absorbs all the information, though she can't repeat what she hears.

Parva and I took Roxy for a walk when we got home. Roxy was very glad to see us since we had been gone all morning. I decided to make it an extra-long walk, to delay the inevitable. But when we finally got home, mom said, "Okay, girls, it's time to get in the car."

I knew I couldn't delay any longer. Both of us went upstairs to brush our teeth first, grab a stuffed animal (my idea) and then joined my mom downstairs. My mom gave me a pill to take to calm me down.

It was a pretty quiet ride to my mom's office, so she put on some classical music to break the silence. We live in a small town, so it didn't take long to get there. Parva was overwhelmed with all the equipment and big machinery. With a deep breath, I got in the big chair and held on to Parva's hand. My mom started with x-rays. She showed Parva what my teeth looked like internally. Parva was shocked! I opened my mouth and Parva looked in my mouth. Then the hygienist started cleaning. Parva was afraid of the sound (so was I), but my mom kept reassuring her. After the cleaning, she checked my teeth for cavities. I had one, so my mom went through the process of filling that and explaining to Parva what she was doing and why. I hated the Novocain shot but did my best not to cry out.

Next it was Parva's turn. They wanted to take extra x-rays of her mouth because it was a unique opportunity to study a Cro-Magnon tooth structure. Fortunately, x-rays don't hurt, so Parva didn't really care. However, when they went to clean her teeth, the hygienist had a real challenge because the contours of Parva's teeth were very different from mine. Parva was getting squirmy even though I was holding her hand, and so the hygienist had to work quickly and efficiently. When my mom did the exam, it was her turn to be astounded. Parva's teeth were so different from our own! She wished she could study them more but didn't want to exploit the friendship. Parva did have all her adult teeth and four cavities. My mom gave her a pill, and then went to work filling the cavities. The sound of the drill was very stressful for Parva until the medicine kicked in, then she didn't care. I thought it was a good thing we had a big lunch, because we would not be able to eat much for supper with our sore mouths and all.

The medicine made Parva extra sleepy because she wasn't used to taking any drugs, so we helped her up to the bedroom and both of us took a nap when we got home. Rather than relying on stuffed animals, Roxy flopped on the bed with us, and soon all three of us were out like a light.

Chapter 8

Dear Diary,
 Parva is still sleeping. Maybe my mom gave her too much medicine. I bet she has never taken medicine in her entire life before. Something weird is happening with my parents. In the beginning, my mom said Parva could stay however long was 'necessary', and my dad said we needed to take her back home immediately. Now they have flip-flopped. My mom thinks we should be taking her home and my dad thinks she should stay as long as she wants! Parents! I am just glad I have a friend this summer, though I wish Junie was here to share the experience with me. Glad the tooth adventure is over!

I had a quiet evening with my parents as Parva continued to sleep. Periodically, one of us would go up to check on her to make sure she was still breathing or to see if she was awake, but all was quiet. My parents and I played some card games and talked and just 'connected' with each other.
 Another week passed with bike riding, game playing, going to the park, fishing and looking at books. Then my mom came up with another 'bright' idea. She wanted

Parva to get her eyes tested. She has a good friend who is an optometrist that she trusts. She had lunch with her the other day and attempted to explain the situation to her. The doctor said that Parva would need to know the primary color words and the letters of the alphabet to do the exam properly, so my dad has a new mission. Every night he has been going over colors with Parva and the letters of the alphabet. When they have done pictures in the past, he has never forced her to repeat after him. But now with the color words and letters he is, and she is a little confused. English is very hard for her. I think my dad is going to have to go into the exam and interpret what she is saying, because it is not always clear to the normal ear. For example, the word 'yellow' is often pronounced 'ELO' by Parva.

I don't wear glasses, nor does my mom, but my dad does. What, really, can Parva see? Will glasses make a difference? How will she react? In her world, it is a lot darker than in ours. Will that make a difference with her vision? I even wonder what her parents would think about it.

I have been trying to help Parva with her lessons by pointing out letters and colors during our Roxy walks. Mom has put up more labels in the house. Parva does get confused between lowercase and capital letters. Different shades of color are a challenge as well. She can identify 'red', for example, but what about 'red-orange' or 'red-violet'? She wants to know if these are 'red', too. I guess when you grow up with all of this you are not bothered by these distinctions, but if it is brand new to you, it can be very confusing. Blue is blue, but then there is sky blue, robin's egg blue, and violet blue.

Dr Bryce is my eye doctor, too, though I don't go very often because I don't need to. She and my mom are long-time friends. Though I know my mom tried to prepare Dr Bryce for Parva, the doctor still did a double take when introduced, although she quickly recovered. All of us went to the appointment. The optometrist started by looking in Parva's eyes with a light. She told us that the eye structure was remarkably similar. Then began the laborious task of determining what Parva could see. This is where my dad had to interpret. Parva started getting squirmy from fatigue, but, in the end, it was decided that glasses would be of benefit to her. A prescription was determined, and then we went over to optical to find a pair of glasses. Mom and dad let me take the lead on this. Because of the shape of Parva's head, we had to go adult-sized glasses, and I was looking for 'cute' ones that would fit her personality. After having her try on many that didn't work, I finally found a pair that was perfect! Parva didn't really understand what was going on, but giggled when I found the pair I liked and expressed my joy. The optician explained it would take a week – a whole week! – before the glasses came in. Mom paid for them and then we went out to dinner to celebrate. I didn't finish all my supper, so was able to bring home a 'doggy bag' for Roxy. All in all, it was a great day.

***

Parva had seen dad work outside on and off since she had been living with us. When we got up the next morning, she wanted to know if she could help my dad work outside. I wasn't sure what she could do safely, but she was eager and had learned so much already. At breakfast, I told dad that Parva wanted to help him outside. He grinned (because I never offer to help) and said, "Of course you can help!"

My mom suggested that I read one of the books from Mrs Ferguson's list since Parva would be otherwise occupied. She also said she would make chocolate chip cookies for all of her 'crew' in the afternoon.

So, dad and Parva went to work in the garden, doing tilling and planting. Dad showed her how to work the machine, showed her different types of seed, and the importance of watering after planting. She held the ladder for him while he climbed up to clean the gutters, and even let her climb the ladder once to see out over the neighborhood. They pulled dandelions and other weeds (some good plants accidently got pulled up as well by Parva and had to be replanted!), and they reseeded bare spots in the lawn. Parva didn't understand how little grass seeds could sprout into a lush lawn, so my dad put together a little experiment for her that he remembered doing when he was young. He took a Styrofoam cup, and they put dirt in it about three-quarters full. Carefully with marker they drew a smiley face on the cup. Then they planted grass seed in the cup. They covered the seeds with a little dirt.

Dad explained that it needed water and sun every day and that it was Parva's responsibility. Parva decided to name her cup 'GUS' from a character in one of her favorite books. She dutifully watered Gus and made sure Gus got sun as he smiled at her every day. Soon Gus started sprouting green hair! Parva was thrilled beyond thrilled! After a time, dad told her to give Gus a 'haircut', and though she was reluctant, she did, and to her surprise, Gus' hair grew back! It was a great lesson for her.

While dad and Parva were outside working, Roxy and I were curled up on the couch, reading book number two. It was quiet in the house, and I actually got quite a bit of reading done, though I did daydream a bit... thinking about what it would be like taking Parva to grade 5 with me. How would the other students react to Parva? Would they accept her? What if we weren't put in the same class? That would be disastrous. Surely, my parents wouldn't let that happen. My reverie was broken by mom bringing me a tuna sandwich for lunch and a glass of iced tea. I ate while I refocused on my book. It wasn't long before the smell of cookies assaulted my nose. Yum! When I could hardly stand the smell any more, mom called all of us in and we sat down to warm cookies and cold milk. What a treat!

Chapter 9

"Mom," I yelled. "Your cell phone is ringing!"

"Thanks, Myka, but you don't have to yell! I'm just in the next room! Hello? Yes? They are? How late are you open? We will be there. Thank you."

Mom turned to us. "Good news, Myka and Parva! The glasses are in! We can pick them up this afternoon. I will pick up you two around three, okay?"

"Yes!" I said excitedly. "We will be ready."

Parva just looked at me. I smiled, and so she smiled back. She is in for a big surprise, I thought to myself. I can't wait.

Mom went off to work, and now that Parva knows her basic colors, dad is teaching her to play UNO, so we played a few games of that. Parva checked on Gus, we took Roxy for a walk, then we went to Juba Park to play on the equipment (mostly the slides), and while we were there the ice cream truck came by. I just happened to have some money in my pocket, so we treated ourselves to some ice cream, which Parva can never get enough of. But she ALWAYS eats it too fast and gets brain freeze, no matter how many times I tell her to slow down. We skipped some rocks at the pond on the way home, and I am trying to teach

Parva how to skip with her body, but she is top heavy, so it is difficult for her.

Mom picked us up and off we went to the doctor's office. I think Parva thought she was going to have to name more colors, and she was nervous that dad did not come with us. When we got there, we walked into the optician side of the office and Parva sat down, just waiting. Then they called her name, which startled her. I wish we had videotaped her expression when they first put the glasses on her! Her expression was one of complete amazement. She took them off and looked at them, smelled them and touched them to her face. Then put them back on her face with some help. We have never seen Parva cry (can she?), but she got very emotional and ran over to my mom and buried her face in her lap. It seemed like she was scared and excited at the same time but didn't know how to express it. My mom asked her if she could see pretty good, and she nodded her head 'yes' so violently, I thought she was going to break her neck! She wanted to touch, smell and experience everything all over again. She even looked at me differently and touched my face. Everything is tactile for her. She clearly was delighted but overwhelmed. We were all so happy for her. She wanted to hurry home so she could show dad, and she also said to me, "LOK MIRR."

I said, "They have a mirror here," and took her over to the mirror in the optician department so she could see herself. She stared for a long time. Then she began to giggle, and I knew everything was going to be okay. Even

Dr Bryce came out of the office to join in the celebration. It was a great ride home, because Parva was seeing things as they really are for the first time... in all the brightness of their natural colors. She was very, very happy.

Dad was in his study when we pulled into the driveway, and Parva had her seatbelt off in a flash and beat us all into the house and raced into his office to show him. She was so proud to show off her new glasses, and dad congratulated her. He thought her reading would go much faster now that her vision was improved. I thought her balance would be even better on the bike. We celebrated with a special dinner that night, and Parva never stopped grinning the whole time!

Since Parva had spent a day with dad, she was now eager to spend a day with mom. As an only child, I was not used to sharing my parents, but I was kinda getting used to it. Mom was going to go grocery shopping, which is not my favorite thing to do anyway, but Parva wanted to go with mom, so I really didn't care. So, they got up early the next morning to go to Fisher's.

At lunch that afternoon, my mom told me and my dad what happened. Parva was overwhelmed at all the food in one place. Unfortunately for mom, they started in the fruits and vegetable section; unfortunate, because Parva did not want to move on! She recognized some of the root vegetables and fruits and wanted to touch them to her face and smell them. People around them were looking at her kinda weird, I guess. She thought every vegetable and fruit was special and worthy of touch and smell. The only real mishap was when Parva couldn't resist and took a big bite out of a juicy peach! My mom had to explain to her that things were just to look at and put in the cart, and that they had to be paid for first. So, into the basket went a peach with a bite in it! Once my mom FINALLY got her out of the fresh fruits and vegetables, they next got hung up in the meat section. Parva wasn't interested in chicken or pork or hotdogs or lunchmeat, but oh, was she excited to see the pieces of beef on display. Guess the red meat brought back memories. She put that up to her face to touch and smell, too, and my mom had to watch her carefully that she didn't bite into the raw meat!

They finally made it through the rest of the store and mom got through her shopping list, but it took a long time before they finally got home. She made steak for dinner, with Parva's being very rare, and she was in heaven. Before heading to bed, Parva and I took a shower that night, separately now, and put on warm, clean pajamas. Parva especially likes soft underwear and soft pajamas. And, of course, a soft bed. She usually wakes up earlier than me and now goes downstairs on her own, where my dad, who is an early riser, is also usually up. It is good bonding time for them. He makes her hot chocolate while he has a cup of coffee, and they watch the sunrise together. Then they usually read together until my mom, and I roll out of bed.

Chapter 10

For a few days after Parva got her glasses, things were basically routine. She liked to be outdoors, get new words for things, was beginning to spell things with my dad's help, and recognize colors pretty consistently. She wasn't always easy to understand yet, as I think some letters were just difficult for her to pronounce; but she sure tried really hard to communicate. Our family got better at interpreting her speech, though an outsider would really struggle. One night at dinner, Parva seemed unusually quiet. In fact, my parents were wondering if maybe she wasn't feeling good. Suddenly, she blurted out, "SEE MEMA." There was silence for a moment around the table.

I finally said, "Parva, do you want to go see your mom?"

She shook her head 'yes'. The time had come when Parva wanted to go back home. I don't think any of us saw that coming.

"Of course," dad replied. "Myka will take you home. It has been a joy having you here, but you must miss your family."

I was shocked. I had pictured her going to school with me and everything. My mom told her we would put together some things for her to take with her. I turned to my dad. "When do I have to take her back?"

"Well, let's see. Today is Friday. We will need to do some shopping. Why don't you plan on taking her back Monday? That will give us some time to say goodbye and get things organized."

I fought tears.

Dear Diary,

A truly sad day. Parva wants to go home. I understand, but it still hurts. She has been my friend all summer and I wanted her to go to fifth grade with me. I wanted her to meet Junie and all my friends, and we would have such a grand time together. But now she misses her family and wants to return to her world. As much as I will miss her, I would not want to go with her.

Over the weekend, we did all our favorite things, ate all our favorite foods, and took long walks with Roxy. I couldn't believe I had to take her back home, but her family probably missed her, too. Sunday night, after she was sound asleep, I did something I haven't done in a long time. I went to my parents' bedroom and crawled in bed with them and just sobbed. They were very understanding, but firm. They said it was good she came to the decision on her own. My mom said it was likely the trip to the grocery store that triggered her longing for her own family. My dad said I had to be brave for Parva's sake and that I would remember her forever.

My mom put together a backpack of soft pajamas, comfy underwear, toothbrush and toothpaste, and scented soap for Parva, her most favorite things from our world. At eleven thirty a.m., my dad drove us to the portal. I told him not to wait; I would walk home after getting Parva settled, as I wanted time to myself. When the portal opened at noon, Parva said goodbye to my dad and Parva, and I stepped through the portal.

It was quiet and dim. We turned to the right on the path and began to walk toward Parva's family cave. We met no one on our walk, heard no sounds except the gurgling brook right by the portal and saw no critters. After walking about thirty minutes by my watch, we turned the last bend in the path and found... nothing. Parva's family cave was empty! But oh, what a mess was left behind! There was trash everywhere! Empty bread bags, discarded soup and chili cans, and empty jars of peanut butter and jelly lay all over the place. Empty boxes of spaghetti, crackers and ramen noodles were lying in the dirt. Empty cans of Sprite, Coke and 7-Up were randomly tossed throughout the campsite. Broken spaghetti jars, pickle jars and condiment containers were haphazardly in the mess. All the food I had ever brought them, including milk cartons that they kept cool in the clear stream and cream containers and yogurt cartons, clogged the previously pristine waters. There was pollution everywhere I looked! What had I done? I was horrified! It even took me a while to notice that the people weren't there, even though that was the first thing Parva noticed. I checked the coal fire pit... not even close to warm. It had been a while since Parva's family had been here. Oh no! Now what? Parva was very distraught. She began to make sounds I never heard her make. Kind of like keening sounds. I had to decide. Though I felt like crying myself, I had to be the one in charge, as I felt responsible for this mess. I told Parva we were going to go back to my house and talk to my parents to see what we should do. I couldn't handle this on my own. So, we went back through the portal and walked home.

My mom was doing dishes and saw us coming before we got to the house. She admits she was angry with me at first for bringing Parva back home with me, because she thought I was being selfish. But then when we got closer, she saw our body language and our faces and knew something was wrong. She called for my dad, and they met us in the kitchen. After hugs all round, the story spilled out.

"What do you mean, her family 'is gone'?" my dad asked. "Where could they go? Could they have gone through the portal, too?"

"I doubt it," I said. "We would have heard about it."

"We have to find them," mom said. "Though I admit I don't know how to do that."

Parva was clearly upset, and my dad was the calmest among us, so he spent extra time with her to ease her fears. He talked gently to her and told her we would do all we could to find her family. He read to her like he always used to do, made her hot chocolate, and comforted her. In the meantime, I went to my mom's room, sobbing and saying it was all my fault.

"What do you mean, Myka? How can her family moving away be your fault?"

"Well, I was the one feeding them. I was the one taking care of them. They were my responsibility. Once Parva came out into our world, I never once brought them any more food! I was having too much fun with Parva and never thought again about them. They probably starved to death. And I certainly never thought about how their beautiful environment would get trashed!"

"Slow down, Myka. Let's take the second thing first. What happens when we empty a can of beans?"

"We throw it in the garbage bin."

"Then what happens?"

"Dad takes the garbage down to the curb."

"Then what?"

"The garbage truck picks it up."

"And takes it where?"

"I don't know. Somewhere to dump it off."

"Okay. So, we have a whole system in place to remove our garbage. Does that system exist in Parva's world?"

"No."

"They didn't know what to do because they never had garbage like that before, so they just threw it on the ground because they have no system in place. They didn't even have garbage bags to put empties into. When you try to do a good thing, you must think through the consequences. Is there something they need besides the obvious? Is there some education they need to help them... like Parva needing to learn colors before her eye exam? You must think ahead, Myka. You can't just barge forward with a plan. You must think of the details. So, what can we do now, after the fact, to fix this problem?"

"We can go clean up the trash and make it look like it did before," Myka sobbed.

"Right. And all of us will do it together. That solves the environmental problem. Now, for finding Parva's family, that's a different issue..."

"I think I starved them, mom. They are probably dead." And at this realization, I began to cry even harder.

"Hold on a minute," my mom cautioned. "Weren't they doing fine before you got there? Weren't they eating and surviving before you even met Parva?"

"Well, yes."

"They might have just gone back to their former ways once you stopped supplying them food that wasn't from their century anyway. Didn't you tell me the brothers would hunt? They probably went back to hunting/gathering. But maybe they had to do it in a different place because of the pollution our twenty-first century food brought into their environment."

"But how do we find them?"

"I don't know. But first we need to clean up the environment and then we will regroup. Agreed?"

"Agreed."

"Go wash your face with warm water since you've been crying so hard and let me talk to your father tonight. We'll figure out a plan. We're a family, and we'll stick together on this."

Chapter 11

Mom and dad talked long into the night. I was exhausted from crying so hard and Parva was very sad. Even Roxy was restless because she sensed something wasn't right. It was a bad night all round. Two days later, my mom, dad, Parva and me all piled into the car with the wagon and a bunch of garbage bags and gloves. We were going to clean the environment first, because we felt that was the easiest of the two problems to tackle. Parva didn't exactly understand, but dad tried to explain that we would look for her family at another time. My mom was really scared, because she had never been through the portal before. I am not sure she really wanted to go, but she had said we would do this as a family, so she kinda was stuck. We didn't want anyone to really notice us, but, come on, four people and a wagon are not easy to blend into the scenery. We decided to go in shifts. Parva and I went first. Then, in a little bit, my dad shoved the wagon through the portal. Then the plan was for him and mom to follow the wagon. The wagon came and Parva and I waited for mom and dad... and waited... and waited. They weren't coming! Maybe they changed their minds! I was just about to go back 'out' to see what was happening, when in they came. Mom looked a little pale. Apparently, she was having second, third and fourth thoughts about this plan, and dad had to convince her that going through the portal was the right thing to do. I have never known my mom to be indecisive before; but then again, this was a most unusual circumstance. At first, no one said anything. We could all hear mom breathing hard, and I hoped she wasn't going to collapse or something. But then dad said quietly, "Okay, we all know why we are here. Parva and Myka, why don't you lead us to the trash?"

So, Parva and I, holding hands and me also pulling the wagon with the empty garbage bags and gloves, led the way down the familiar path. Mom and dad followed us, also holding hands. We kinda looked like a mini parade. Mom kept whispering how quiet and peaceful it was, and dad just shook his head in agreement. I kept looking at my watch, knowing that it took about thirty minutes to get to Parva's family's old cave. We followed the final curve and there it was, trash and all. Mom and dad gasped at the same time. I fought back tears – again. We all put on a pair of gloves and started to clean things up. Dad handled the broken glass; mom went to the stream and Parva, and I went to the cave. With the four of us working together, it didn't take all that long to get things cleaned up. We did fill four garbage bags, though, which we piled onto the wagon. Dad asked Parva where the trail led, and she told him to more "TEES". He asked her whether she thought her family went that way, and she emphatically shook her head 'no'. "TAIL TOP AT TEES," which dad interpreted as the trail stops at the trees. Since we were only going to tackle one mission at a time, it was best to head home now.

We started for the portal and our walk was a little slower because of the full wagon. When we got to the turn for the portal, dad asked Parva where the trail went in this direction. Parva's eyes got really big behind her glasses, and she ran to my mom and buried her face in her legs. That was odd. Dad reached out for her, and she must have thought he was going to take her down that trail or something, because she started making funny noises and began to run away in the opposite direction! Dad was stunned! She had never been afraid of him before. Mom reached out before Parva could get very far and pulled her into an embrace. Mom said to Parva, "Let's go home," and holding hands, the two of them went through the portal just like that.

Dad and I just stared at each other like 'what just happened?' and we felt we had missed out on something. Dad just shrugged and said, "Guess it's a mystery to be solved later! Now, how do we get this garbage through the portal and then ourselves?"

Soon, we were in the car heading back home. The garbage bags were placed in the twenty-first century garbage pick-up service, and we were all eating ice cream that dad had stopped to get. One problem solved, one to go. How in the world do we find Parva's family? This time, we had a family meeting with Parva included. Dad said he needed to understand Parva's reaction to him when he asked about the path. Why was she so scared? I didn't know the answer. It was never something we talked about, though I had noticed that whenever I visited her in her world, she would only go so far with me on the trail and then she would stop. Every time. I told my dad about this. She was always reluctant to go any further.

"Parva," Dad said in a gentle voice, "you said that if you follow the trail one way it leads to trees and then the trail stops. Right?"

Parva shook her head 'yes'.

"Where does the trail go if you follow it in the other direction?"

Silence.

"Parva," Dad said quietly, "I am only trying to understand your world better so that I can help you find your family. Don't be scared. We are here to help you."

Without warning, Parva got up and went over to mom and sat in her lap, which she had never done. Dad couldn't believe it. Actually, none of us could.

Mom hugged her and said, "It's okay, Parva. You can tell us." Mom had no idea what was going on in Parva's head, only that she was nervous and shaking. Mom felt she needed to talk and wanted to encourage her.

After another long period of silence, Parva blurted out, "MEMA, NO. PARVA, NO."

What did this mean? Clearly it was important, and she was very distressed even saying it.

Dad pushed, "Parva can't go on the trail?"

Parva said again, this time even louder, as if dad hadn't heard her the first time, "MEMA, NO. PARVA, NO."

Mom was the one who figured it out. She turned to Parva and said, "You and your mom don't go on that trail, do you? You must stop."

Parva smiled at her understanding and shook her head 'yes'.

Mom said to Dad and me that she thought females were not allowed down that way, only males. Females probably gathered food, like fruit and roots, while the males hunted. That's probably why she reacted the way she did at the grocery store!

I then asked Parva, "Parva, you have brothers?"

She shook her head 'yes'.

"They go down that trail, don't they?"

Again, she shook her head 'yes'.

"When I saw them, Parva, they had an animal – meat – with them. Did they get that at the end of that trail?"

I thought her neck was going to break when she shook her head 'yes', this time.

My father then realized that the trail led to the hunting ground and that females were not allowed. "Parva had probably been taught this early on," he explained. "No wonder she was so afraid! She thought I was going to make her go down that path which her parents had trained her not to do. It makes sense now! But if her parents are not to the right of the portal, they must have gone on the path to the left. There are no other choices."

My mom's eyes got real big and she exclaimed, "You mean WE'RE going to have to go into the hunting grounds to find her family? I don't like the sound of that at all! I am not sure that is safe for any of us."

"Woah," whistled dad. "This is getting complicated. I am not sure how to do this. Maybe we need to involve the police or something. I really don't know what we're getting into."

"No!" I said. "We'll handle it just like we have done every challenge – as a family. We can figure this out, dad. We just need some time to think this through. Please don't call anyone yet. Let's see what we can figure out on our own, as a family. We are in this together – you always say that to me!"

"She's right," said mom. "We are a family. Let's give it some time and think on it. Parva is an important part of our family, and we need to do what we can for her."

Chapter 12

All of us had a sleepless night. I had a dream about being chased by weird animals that I had never seen before. They were all after me and I was having a hard time getting away. Mom and dad said they had similar dreams. The unknown can be scary. And poor Parva didn't even know where her real family was! What a mess. This was not how I expected my summer to go; and it certainly had more adventure to it than any book Mrs Ferguson could assign! I kept trying to think about ways to go into the hunting area safely so we would not be a target for either Parva's family (accidently, of course) or for any wild beast. Guns were not safe because we didn't know anything at all about the environment we were going into or where Parva's family was. Knives? Same problem. We needed something more simple but effective. Then, on a day when I was supposed to be cleaning my bedroom, I thought of it. I figured out how we could safely go into the hunting environment to find Parva's family. I was so excited!

Though reluctant, my family agreed to my plan, and we were going to go to the portal the next day since mom didn't have to go to work. My dad found a long stick in the back yard. My mom got an empty bread wrapper, and an empty baked bean can. I peeled the label off the can and grabbed dad's duct tape. We all put on long pants and long sleeves just in case we ran into something unpleasant. We loaded up Parva's backpack with personal items for her (including an extra pair of glasses), and put some extra blankets, a pillow, and some soft towels in the wagon. All of that went in the car and then the four of us piled in and away we went to the portal. I was excited to see if my plan would work, but I think my parents were skeptical. It was explained to Parva that she was going to go into the hunting area, but that my dad, a male, would be with her, so that made it okay. A stretch? Yes, but we had to convince her to go with us in some way.

We tumbled through the portal and acclimatized ourselves to the low light. Clearly, Parva was nervous. I took the long stick from my dad and the bread wrapper from my mom. With the duct tape, I put the wrapper on the stick at the top like a flag or pennant so that if there was a breeze, it would fill with air. Then I took the can and turned it upside down and placed it on top of the stick. If there was sun, it would reflect off that; it would also twirl in the wind. I had to pull a little on Parva's hand and dad had to push her a little from the back to get her to turn left onto the path from the portal. It was so ingrained in her not to go in that direction that it was hard for her to do so. I took the lead with the stick, holding Parva's hand slightly behind me. Mom and dad held hands and pulled the wagon. We walked on the dirt trail for about ten minutes when there was a curve which opened to a whole new scene.

Instead of trees, rock formations and gurgling water, there was tall grass everywhere. My mom and dad could barely see over it, it was so high. Parva and I couldn't see anything except the grass. I had to hold the stick way up. My dad offered to carry it for me, but I was determined to do it myself. Surprisingly, there was sun on this side of the portal and an occasional breeze. I wouldn't have expected either, but this whole world is weird to me. I thought that her family would recognize the bread wrapper and be drawn to the reflecting can if they were even close enough to see it – they would not only recognize it as artificial, but as something I had previously brought them to eat. I also hoped whatever animals found us would be afraid of it and stay away! It was of no value as a weapon, but I hoped its unfamiliarity to the animals was enough of a deterrent.

My heart was beating very fast. My hands were all sweaty. My family was risking a lot for Parva's family. And all of this because I investigated a shiny thing one summer day that felt like eons ago. Junie just wouldn't believe this story. We walked slowly, not wanting to unnecessarily disturb the wrong thing in this weird world. I heard dad whisper that fifteen minutes had passed, yet nothing had changed. Parva and I could still see nothing except tall grass. We kept walking, then suddenly there was this loud, bird-like sound close by that made the three twenty-first century people nearly jump out of their skins. The three of us instinctively crouched down and tucked our heads. A little giggle erupted. Dad asked, "What was that?"

The sound happened again, and this time we all realized it came from Parva! The bird-like sound was SO realistic, and none of us had ever heard it before.

Dad asked Parva, "Where did you learn that?"

"MEMA."

"When did you learn it from your mom?" he questioned.

"ITL," she explained.

"Why did your mom teach you that sound when you were little?"

"UBL," she explained.

"Well, this is certainly a good time to use it, because we are in trouble," dad chuckled. "But you could have warned us!" he laughed softly.

Dad announced another fifteen minutes had gone by. Parva emitted another bird sound. This time, there was a responding sound from far, far away. Parva grinned. Dad told her to do it again, and we heard the answering sound again. Dad and mom were both encouraged but reminded us to keep up our guard. More time passed, more sounds emitted, and we kept getting closer and closer, and then...

Parva ran to her family, who just stared at her. Here she was in twenty-first century clothes, with glasses, and running to hug her family. And who were all these others with her? It was Parva's mom who finally broke the spell and reached out for her daughter. It was beautiful. The three of us were crying, even my dad. My mom got up her nerve and brought the wagon up to the staring family. She showed all the things that were in the wagon. Then she gently asked Parva's mom if she could hold her baby. Parva somehow communicated to her mom that it would be okay. My mom took the baby, and after hugging him, laid him gently in the wagon amid the soft pillows and blankets. Then she showed Parva's mom how she could pull the wagon with the baby in it instead of always carrying the baby. The grin on Parva's mom's face was the best of all as understanding dawned. I was so happy my little wagon was going to go back in time to spend its days in another world. Then we said our goodbyes, which were full of tears and hugs and broken English.

Parva's dad told one of her brothers to lead us out of the grasslands, which we were grateful for. I had thought maybe we could follow the bent grass we had made when we walked through, but having an escort was even safer. We had walked quite a while, so it took some time to get back to the dirt trail. We thanked the brother, who didn't understand our words, and we started breathing normally again.

"I am going to miss her so much!" I said. "It was like having an instant sister."

"I think we're all going to miss her," replied my mom. "She brought a lot of joy into our lives."

"Time to go home to our world," sighed dad. "There is nothing for us here. We've done all we can."

Chapter 13

At dinner that night, we were all a little subdued. Then dad said, "You know, Myka, it was a good thing it was you who found that portal and not someone else."

"What do you mean?" I asked.

"Well, someone else may have taken advantage of the situation. For example, they may have exploited Parva and her family or used up the rich resources in the environment. You just wanted to be a friend."

"I didn't do all good, dad. There are mistakes I made. Like the trash, and not feeding them after Parva came to live with us."

"True, but you didn't do that intentionally, and you made up for it. I worry about the people who are out to do harm right from the beginning. I worry about the wrong people going through the portal."

"Do you think we need to tell someone about it?" asked mom. "To prevent a misuse in the future?"

"I don't know the answer," admitted dad. "I need to think some more about it. I am just uncomfortable ending things here. I don't want Parva or her family or her environment to be in any danger."

That night, I had nightmares. Mean people had gotten through the portal and were cutting down trees, sucking up all the water, chasing after all the animals and laughing at Parva and her family. I tried to stop everything in my dream, but they chained me up and put a rag in my mouth to keep me quiet! I couldn't even reach out to my parents! Roxy was barking in the distance, and I was afraid they were going to hurt her, too. I woke up all hot and sweaty, only too glad to find out it was just a dream.

Dad called a family meeting after breakfast. It had to be a short one because mom had to work that day. He said that it was his opinion that we needed to close the portal forever and wanted to know what we thought about that. Mom said she agreed. I said no that I wanted to take Junie there to show her Parva's world! Dad challenged me to think about who Junie would want to invite, and then who that person would want to invite, and then who that person would want to invite, and then who...

"But it doesn't have to go like that!" I argued. "It could just be me and Junie!"

"Myka," Dad said, "you are almost a teenager. You have a lot of friends. Word would get around. It would be hard to keep it a secret. There could be danger for Parva if it got out. Can you look ahead for a minute? I understand that you want to show it to Junie, but is that the safest and best decision for Parva?"

I admit to pouting. I know my dad was right, but I didn't want him to be right. "All right," I said, "but can I at least take a few pictures with my phone, first?"

"Fair enough," agreed dad.

Mom asked the practical question of HOW he intended to close the portal forever.

"I have the start of a plan, but I need to research it a little bit more. I will work on the plan today after Myka takes her pictures."

Dear Diary,

Something weird happened today. My dad allowed me to go back through the portal to take some pictures of Parva's world. I rode my bike up to Fisher's and at the appropriate time went through the portal just fine. I first took a picture of the beautiful bubbling brook. But when I checked to see how the photo turned out, it was just a blank shot! So, I took another one... blank again! I took a picture of a tree... blank! What is going on? Every picture I tried to take wouldn't take. I was incredibly frustrated. Finally, I just gave up and tried to just memorize it in my brain. When I got outside the portal, I took a picture of the front of Fisher's and it was a perfect shot, so it wasn't the cell phone's problem. Weird.

At supper that night, I told my parents what happened with the camera, and they were both surprised and not surprised at the same time. They reminded me that it is a different world and that things are not the same as in our world. Dad also explained his plan for closing the portal. Mom thought it would be too 'obvious', but dad said that we had been pushing a wagon through the portal as well as garbage bags and ourselves and no one ever said anything or stopped us, so he thought this plan should be okay, too. I agreed to help him, even if it made me sad.

Since time of day didn't matter (we weren't going through the portal), we decided to initiate the plan early in the morning because there would be fewer people milling around downtown. Dad got me up at five thirty a.m. (yawn!) and we got busy in the garage. I found the two big buckets he requested, and he filled them up halfway with water and put them in the back of the SUV. I found two sets of gloves and a box opener. It took me a while to find some kind of metal stirrer, and lastly, I gave him the shovel. The two bags he had bought yesterday were already in the SUV. We drove to the portal and parked as close as we could. Dad had to carry the buckets of water because they were too heavy for me. He also had to carry the bags he had bought at the store for the same reason. I could carry the gloves, box opener, shovel, and stirrer. He used the box opener to open one bag of dry cement and poured it into one of the buckets. He quickly stirred it and with the shovel started scooping it over the place where the portal usually shines. Then he opened the second bag of dry cement, poured that into the second bucket, stirred it and shoveled it out again over where the area of the portal usually is, and then around the edges. It was messy, but we spread it out and patted it down using our gloved hands. We cleaned everything up and put everything left over into the SUV. My dad had bought quick-drying cement, and it was already starting to harden. We stood around talking for about ten minutes, then my dad stomped with his big boots all around the area, making sure it was solid. We agreed to come back at noon to see if our plan worked.

I was nervous all morning. After taking Roxy for a walk, I tried to read, but kept getting distracted by my own thoughts. Time seemed to creep by. Finally, at eleven fifty a.m., dad said, "Let's roll!" – and I nearly jumped out of my skin! We went down to the portal, getting there a little too early by my watch. We waited until 12.05 p.m., then dad jumped (wish I had a video!) on top of the mound of cement and... nothing happened! He jumped in another section, and again nothing. I tried. Nothing. We did it! We sealed up the portal! As long as the concrete stayed in place, Parva and her family were safe! I had so many mixed emotions! Dad was quite pleased with himself! In fact, he took me – just me – out to lunch!

Two weeks later, Junie FINALLY came home! I screamed when I saw her coming down my street! We met halfway.

"Junie!" I gushed. "You're never going to believe what happened to me this summer..."

www.ingramcontent.com/pod-product-compliance
Lightning Source LLC
LaVergne TN
LVHW041537060526
838200LV00037B/1019